This book is part of
THE LONGMAN BOOK PROJECT

General Editor Sue Palmer
Fiction Editor Wendy Body
Non-fiction Editor Bobbie Neate

Acknowledgements
The author thanks Djavan, Geert, Ruben, Tessa, Amelie, Patty and David Alexander

ADDISON WESLEY LONGMAN LIMITED
Edinburgh Gate, Harlow, Essex CM20 2JE, England
and Associated Companies throughout the World.

First published 1995
ISBN 0 582 12245 7
Fifth impression 1999

Printed in Singapore (JBW)

The publisher's policy is to use paper manufactured from sustainable forests.

When the rain stopped in Natland

by **Alecia McKenzie**

Illustrated by **Guy Parker-Rees**

LONGMAN

Chapter
One

· ·

Tim Lambert lived in a small town in Natland, a country where it rained at least 360 days of the year. He lived with his mother, his sister Cathy and his parrot Callaloo.

Callaloo was a gift from his Aunt Liana who lived in Slushigem, the capital of Natland. Aunt Liana originally came from another land, Chaud'terre, where the sun shone 360 days a year, with five days left over for the hurricane. Each year, the hurricane had a different name. The last one had been called Stormin' Norman and it had blown away many of the houses in Chaud'terre, Aunt Liana had told Tim.

It was summertime now in Natland, although you wouldn't have guessed it from the rain. People walked around with huge umbrellas and rubber boots, splish-splashing about. The children mostly stayed indoors, looking out of the window and waiting for a chance to go out and play.

Tim spent part of his time helping his mother in her flower shop and his grandfather in his shoe-repair shop. But, mostly, he sat daydreaming about the fair. Every summer in Natland, a big fair came to Slushigem with at least fifty rides, their owners hoping against hope that this would be a sunny summer. As soon as there was a lull in the rain, all the children rushed to the fair.

Today Tim was sitting in the living room, drawing pictures of a Big Wheel, when the phone rang.

"'Allo, 'allo," Callaloo said chirpily, as he always did.

"Oh be quiet, bird-brain, you talk too much," Tim told him.

· · · · · · · ·

Usually he was kind to the parrot but today he was in a bad mood
because of the rain.

Rain, rain, rain and more rain. Would it never stop? He went to
answer the phone. "Hello, Lamberts' residence, may I help you?"
he said all in one breath, as Mama had taught him.

"Hello, Mr Lamberts-Residence. How are you?" It was Aunt
Liana.

"Oh, Auntie, it never stops raining, and I'm never going to get
to the fair. It's going to be over and I'll have to wait a whole year
again."

"No, you won't. It will stop raining soon. I can feel it in my bones, although they are not what they used to be because all this rain is giving me rheumatism," Aunt Liana said. "But I bet we'll have some sun in a day or two, and then you and Cathy can come and spend the whole weekend here. We'll go to the fair and have a little party afterwards. But why don't you do something else in the meantime? Draw some pictures, help Grandpa or something."

"That's all I've been doing," Tim sighed. "I have so many pictures now that Grandpa said I deserve to have my own art gallery."

"Ah, stop feeling so bad. Just think of all the rides you'll go on, all the candy-apples you'll eat when you come to the fair. The longer you wait, the better they will taste. How's Cathy?"

"She's gone to singing lessons. She is always singing and then Callaloo starts, too," Tim answered. He started singing over the phone to Aunt Liana, in a high-pitched voice, imitating Cathy. Then he sang in Callaloo's screechy tones, "THE SUN WILL COME OUT TOMORROW, BET YOUR BOTTOM DOLLAR, SOMETHING OR OTHER ..."

Aunt Liana laughed. "You have a lovely voice, Tim. I'll have to tell your mother to let you take opera lessons."

"Aarghh!" Tim said. "Do you want to speak to Mama? She's in the shop, I'll call her. Bye, Auntie Liana."

His mother was busy wrapping a bouquet of tulips for Mrs Visan from up the road. Every Tuesday Mrs Visan, a white-haired lady full of jokes about her aches and pains, came to get her tulips. She was just telling Tim's mother about her fall last Friday. "Broke my glasses. But what can you expect? All these old bones have got so stiff. I need to borrow some new muscles from young Tim there."

She winked at Tim as he came into the flower shop, and he smiled shyly back. He liked Mrs Visan. Grandpa was always saying she was a very nice lady. She put talcum powder in her shoes before she brought them in to be fixed.

"Mama, Auntie Liana is on the phone."

"All right, I'm just finishing. Thank you Mrs Visan."

Tim stayed in the shop while Mama spoke with Aunt Liana in the back. He liked Grandpa's shop much better than his mother's shop because he couldn't stand the smell of all these flowers. Sometimes the whole town smelled of roses because many of the people in Sprinkleton grew or sold flowers for a living.

His mother returned and started telling him something but was interrupted by Callaloo yelling from the living room, "Weekend in Slushigem. Weekend in Slushigem."

"That parrot, he listens to everybody's conversation," said Mama. "Can't keep a secret in this house. Anyway, you and Cathy can go and spend this weekend in Slushigem with Aunt Liana and Uncle Peter if the weather is good, okay?"

"Yippeeeeeeee. Thank you, Mama. Can I go and tell Grandpa?"

"Yes, but come back by six o'clock, in time for dinner."

Tim quickly put on his jacket and raced up the road to Grandpa's shoe-repair shop. There were three people in line at the counter so he slipped in and went to stand beside Grandpa, who was handing out little square tickets in exchange for the battered, broken-down shoes.

Mr Hicks, tall and thin as a stick, was one of the customers. He was dressed in his striped blue suit, bright green hat and red plastic raincoat. Most people thought he was a bit of a nut, partly because of the way he dressed and partly because he still lived with his parents although he was quite old – thirty-five or so. He told everyone he was a poet and was always trying to corner his neighbours to get them to listen to his awful poetry. Mr Hicks hoped that one day all the schoolchildren in Natland would have to study his poems.

He gave Grandpa a pair of red and yellow platform shoes to be fixed. He was wearing his spare purple pair.

"Shall I dye them black for you?" Grandpa said with a straight face.

"No, no. Of course not," Mr Hicks said somewhat angrily, blinking his beady eyes at Grandpa. "The heel's gone down a bit on the side. Can you put on a bit of leather there?"

"No problem. Come back on Thursday." Grandpa gave Mr Hicks a ticket marked '29' and the thin man clop-clopped out of the shop.

Next was Mrs Plumme, a smiling round-faced lady who was as broad as she was tall. She wore the highest heels in the town, and

everyone kept waiting for her to fall down. But she never did. She sailed through the streets on her high heels seemingly unaware of the dangers of cobblestones.

But it was the cobblestones that brought her often to Grandpa's shop, because they were terrible to high heels. Every few weeks, Grandpa had to put rubber tips on Mrs Plumme's shoes.

Grandpa's shop was very popular in the town because nobody fixed shoes as well as he did. He'd been doing it for about forty years now so he'd got very good at it. Tim liked the smell of leather and glue in the shop but he thought a lot of the shoes deserved to be thrown in the rubbish bin. Even if their old smelly shoes had a million holes, some people still wanted them to be repaired.

When Grandpa was through with the customers, he turned to Tim. "So, why are you looking so pleased with yourself?"

"Cathy and I are going to the fair this weekend, if the rain stops," Tim told him. "Will you drive us to Slushigem, Grandpa?"

"Well, I'll have to think about it," Grandpa teased. "Ah, I don't see why not. I might even come to the fair myself. It's a long time since I've been."

That night, as the rain beat against the windows and washed across the land, Tim dreamed he was at Aunt Liana's house in Slushigem. He and Cathy were playing in the garden among the hundreds of seashells Auntie kept. Every shell had a different sound. He put one to his ear and heard laughter, singing and the sound of steel drums. *"Ta na na na na. Na na. Ta na na na na. Na na. Wave your hands in the air. Act like you just don't care. Wave your hands in the air. Shake your hips if you dare."*

He picked up another shell and heard the music of the fair.

Disco music from the Whirl-a-Twirl. Ghost music from the Tunnel of Horrors. Ding-ding-ding music from the merry-go-round. Tim made a face in his dream. No way would he go on the boring merry-go-round. That was for Cathy. He would go on the Big Wheel, where he could see the whole of Slushigem.

Suddenly, in his dream, he was on the Big Wheel. He smiled, turning his head from left to right and looking at the Glacé Pyramid – the cone-shaped tower with the white ball on top that the Prince of Natland had built in the centre of Slushigem for all the children. On the first sunny day of the year, every child could go to the Glacé Pyramid, take the lift all the way to the top and get free ice cream. But sometimes there was not one sunny day in the whole year.

As Tim looked at the Glacé Pyramid and licked his lips, the Big Wheel jerked, then began spinning faster and faster. Everything was a whirl. He screamed, "Stop, stop. Let me off! Help, Papa!"

Someone grabbed his shoulder and tried to pull him into the sky. It was Mama. "Tim, Tim, you're dreaming. It's okay."

He opened his eyes briefly, said, "Papa?" and went back to sleep.

Chapter
Two

....

Aunt Liana whistled as she went about her work – this into the oven, that into the freezer; this into the cupboard, that into the dishwasher.

Aunt Liana was a caterer, one of the best in Slushigem. Her phone was always ringing, with people asking, "Can you make us a cake for our wedding? Can you make us pies for a birthday party? Can you cook us *poulet à l'estragon* for a big company dinner?" And Aunt Liana would create dishes that made all the neighbours' mouths water. When you turned into the street on which Aunt Liana lived, the first thing you smelled was chickencakebrowniespototasaladpatties. And Aunt Liana also made her own ice cream, mango flavour. It was Tim's favourite.

Today Aunt Liana was busy, preparing dishes for a big wedding party in Floodington, the port city where you could see ships from all over the world. She had already made the cake but now she was creating little hors d'oeuvres of chicken wrapped in *roti* bread. That was a special treat for her customers. When everything was ready, Uncle Peter would transport it all in their van to Floodington.

She wanted to be finished with all the work soon so that she could start getting things ready for Cathy and Tim's visit. They would be in Slushigem tomorrow if the rain stopped. Aunt Liana looked out of the kitchen window. It was still drizzling but the sun was bravely trying to poke through the clouds. What a country! Natland was so different from her own island, where the sun always shone, except when there was a hurricane.

Chaud'terre was a country in the Caribbean Sea, miles and miles from Natland. She had met Uncle Peter in India, where they were both travelling at the time, and he had asked her to marry him and come back to Natland. But he hadn't told her about the rain.

"Ah well, into every life a little rain must fall," she said to herself. Just then a shaft of sunlight pushed its way into the kitchen, and just as suddenly was gone.

Aunt Liana turned on the radio to keep her company. She always listened to the ABC world service because she didn't yet fully understand the Nat language. Just then the news was about Israel, Bosnia, the United States and then, amazingly, Natland.

"The Prince of the Natters is very ill," the announcer said. "Doctors say he has caught a rare sickness from eating polluted mussels. Everything in the country is now at a standstill while the people wait to see what will happen. If you plan to travel to

Natland, we advise you to wait for a few days."

"My goodness," Aunt Liana said to herself. She looked out of the window. Everything was at a standstill. Even the raindrops had stopped in mid-air. Then the radio went dead, and the dishwasher stopped and the flames under her pots stopped dancing.

"My goodness," she said again. It was stiller than after a hurricane.

She tried the phone but it wasn't working and when she went to the front door to look out into the street, there was not one person to be seen.

The Prince of Natland was a much-loved man who was only one metre tall. Children especially liked him because he had done a lot for them. When he came to the throne, the first thing he did was to knock down all the tall ugly buildings that had made everyone feel so small. Now all the houses in Natland were people-sized. Gone were the gigantic palaces, the multi-storey glass towers, the ugly tenement blocks that his grandfather had built. Prince Nat made Natland neat. The highest building now was the Glacé Pyramid that gave free ice cream on the first sunny day of the year.

Aunt Liana stopped trying to get anything done and waited for Uncle Peter to come home. When he did, he was whispering.

"Have you heard the news?" he asked.

"Yes," Aunt Liana whispered back. "Poor Prince Nat is ill. Bad mussels. And nothing moves."

"We just have to wait. Perhaps things will start moving tomorrow."

The next day was bright and sunny. It was the warmest and most brilliant day Aunt Liana had ever experienced in Natland. Things were working again in the house, although outside it was still very quiet. The nice weather was good news for Tim and Cathy. They could go to the fair now.

But when she was getting ready to phone Tim's mother, Uncle Peter said there would be no fair.

"No fair? What do you mean?" Aunt Liana asked.

"I heard it on the news this morning. The fair will be closed for as long as the Prince is ill. All the rides have been covered with black plastic."

"But Tim and Cathy can still come here," Aunt Liana suggested. "They can play in the garden."

"Sorry, Li," said Uncle Peter. "But there can't be any traffic on the road while the Prince is ill, so Grandpa can't bring them, and I can't go to fetch them."

"Oh," said Aunt Liana. She didn't know what to do.

Natland had stopped.

Chapter
Three

Prince Nat was cold. He lay in bed shivering with the blanket up to his unshaved chin. It was a gorgeous blanket, in red, yellow, green and blue, and quite warm. His great aunt, who had been Empress in some far away country until there was a revolution, had passed it down to him.

He tried to remember what country she had ruled and been run out of. Faux-terre, Beau-terre? Something like that. He called out to his wife.

"Soo, do you remember – arghhhhhh ..." He didn't finish the sentence as an arrow of pain shot across his stomach.

"What's wrong, dear?" Princess Soo Lian said, rushing in from the other room. She was a tall, slim, beautiful woman, with long black hair, the daughter of the King of Tagore. Prince Nat had rescued her when Tagore had its revolution. For a long time after they got married, people would stare at them everywhere they went because the princess was a good metre taller than Prince Nat.

"Pain, arghhhhhh, oh, oh, oh, quick ..." Prince Nat groaned.

Princess Soo Lian rushed for the pretty porcelain chamber pot that lay in the bathroom, another heirloom from the empress great-aunt. She was just in time as Prince Nat coughed up a stream of green, sour-smelling liquid into the pot.

"Oh, I'm so sorry," he gasped.

"Don't be silly, I'm a doctor, remember?"

She took the priceless pot away and came back with a glass of water and some pills. Prince Nat made a face but said nothing as he took the tablets. He didn't want her to say, "I told you so."

And she *had* warned him not to eat the mussels at that restaurant they'd been to the day before. "That pink sauce on them looks rather funny," she had said. "Why don't you order something else?"

But he'd pouted and ignored her advice. "I want mussels, nothing else."

Now he felt miserable.

"Oh, Soo, I feel so bad. It's the first sunny day and I should be at the Glacé Pyramid giving the children ice cream."

"Don't worry, everyone will understand," she said. "Even princes sometimes get upset stomachs." She bent over and kissed him. "I'm late for work, I have to run. Don't forget to take your pills."

She left the room but came back fifteen minutes later, looking angry.

"Do you know what that idiot has done, Nat? He has declared a week of mourning, as if you'd died or something. And nothing is moving outside. They told me that yesterday he even cut off the electricity and gas all over the country except for in the castle. And today he has had the batteries taken out of our cars. How am I going to get to my patients?"

"What!" Prince Nat yelled. "That cretin, that pompous donkey. Where is he?"

He touched a button beside his bed, and soon they heard heavy footsteps approaching the royal chamber. The door swung open as the Prime Minister, Langi Lalla, entered without knocking. He was a tall heavy man, with deep-set eyes, and just one tuft of hair in the middle of his head.

"Yes, Your Majesty?" he said, a look of false concern on his face.

"What's this I hear about your declaring a week of mourning? Am I dead or something?"

"Well, you're certainly indisposed," Langi Lalla said. "Mussels, was it not?" he covered his mouth with his hand, while his shoulders shook.

"Are you laughing, Langi?" Prince Nat asked.

"Not at all, Your Majesty," the Prime Minister said, wiping tears of merriment from his eyes. "I am worried beyond words about you."

"Okay. So what is this about nothing moving, and preventing our cars from going on the road?"

"Well, Your Majesty, I think the people should have some respect for the monarchy," Langi Lalla said, pulling himself up to his full height and speaking in regal tones. "If the Prince is ill, they can't just expect to go about their business as if nothing had happened."

"Let me decide what people should do when I'm ill, all right, Mister Prime Minister?" Prince Nat said sarcastically. He knew that given half a chance, Langi Lalla would find some way to proclaim himself king. "And put the batteries back in our cars. Soo has to go to work."

"As you like, Your Majesty," Langi Lalla said softly. He spun on his heels and left the room. They were sure they heard him mutter as he went, "A working Princess. What a disgrace!"

Princess Soo shook her head. "That man, he's living in another century, you know. See you this evening." She blew a kiss to Prince Nat and left.

Despite the sunlight coming into the room, Prince Nat shivered again. Langi Lalla always gave him the creeps. What a slimy fellow! He was so two-faced that one never knew what he was really thinking. And that voice! When he wanted something, he could purr like a cat. But when he was angry he brayed like a donkey. How on earth had the people of Natland elected such a man?

Prince Nat pulled the blanket up to his chin again, glancing at the intricate pattern. Where did it come from? What country had Great-Aunt Magaretha been Empress of?

Suddenly he remembered. Chaud'terre. Yes, that was it, Chaud'terre. And she had loved it while she was there. Even after the revolutionaries threw her out, she always wanted to go back. In her old age, when she had got quite weak in the head, she always ranted on about "lovely sunny little Chaud'terre" and she would bore everybody by pulling out her black and white pictures of palm trees and white-sand beaches.

"Never rained there," she always said. "Not a drop." Prince Nat tried to imagine such a place but failed. As his stomach tightened once more into knots, he took another pill and soon went to sleep.

The rain woke him up. The first sunny day had come and gone in Natland and now it was back to the usual greyness, even though it was the middle of summer. As he tried to get out of bed, he felt as if claws were tearing at his belly. "Ohhh," he cried as he fell back against the pillows. Just then Princess Soo Lian came in, her hair and clothes wet from the rain.

"Feeling better?"

"No, your pills don't seem to be working," he said grumpily.

But she seemed not to have heard him. "Langi Lalla has told the people not to go anywhere for four weeks, Nat," she told him.

"He said the doctors predicted you'll be ill for at least that long. What is he talking about? You know, I think we're in for some trouble."

Chapter
Four

"Four weeks!" Tim shouted. "Four whole weeks. In four weeks, school is going to start again, and the fair will be gone."

"Calm down a bit, Tim, it's not the end of the world," his mother said. They had just heard on the news that everything in Natland would remain at a standstill until the Prince was better. The Prime Minister had declared that the Prince wanted things that way and that the police would enforce it.

"Only the police, doctors, firefighters, journalists, chimney sweepers, sanitation workers, postmen, farmers and grocers will be allowed to travel by car or other vehicle," Langi Lalla had said on the radio in his purring voice. Everyone else could only walk around their own neighbourhood.

"What is this?" Tim cried. "Is this a democracy or what?"

His mother looked at him in surprise. Where had he learned to talk like that? But then she remembered. That had been his father's favourite phrase. Tim's father had died three years ago in a car accident, when Tim was eight.

"Don't worry," Mrs Lambert said in a softer voice, swallowing the lump in her throat. "Prince Nat will be better in a couple of days and then everything will be back to normal and you can still go to the fair."

But Tim's grey eyes didn't brighten.

"Go upstairs and tell your sister dinner is ready," his mother said gently, running her hand over his curly brown hair. He went to the foot of the stairs and yelled up, "Dinner is raaaaay-deeee, Cath-eeee."

And Callaloo echoed for a full minute afterwards, "Cath-eeee, Cath-eeee, Cath-eeee, Cath-eeee, Cath-eeee …"

"Shut up, you stupid bird," Tim said. "Or I'll tell Aunt Liana to take you back to Chaud'terre."

Cathy, a slim pretty girl of ten, came running down the stairs, her long brown hair in a ponytail. She had been upstairs listening to that singer La Donna's latest record; she was sure she could sing much better than that with all her lessons.

"Did Aunt Liana call yet?" she asked Tim. "Are we going to the fair?"

"We can't go anywhere for four weeks," he told her. "The Mussel-Prince is still sick."

The next day, Prince Nat and his sickness were the talk of the town. In the bakery, at the butcher's, in the laundromat, at the grocer's, the Natters swapped rumours and stories. Some people were sympathetic while others complained and fumed.

At the main square in Tim's town, people huddled under umbrellas and whispered about what would happen if the Prince died. Would Langi Lalla take over? Would Princess Soo Lian become ruler? Other people didn't care about all that. They were just angry that they couldn't go where they wanted. Mrs Plumme, for instance.

She ran into Tim's mother on the street and stopped to give vent to her rage.

"Imagine," she said, stamping one high-heeled foot. "A little bellyache and the whole country has to come to a full stop. What a nut that Prince Nat is." She stamped her foot again and the heel came off her shoe. "Oh my, oh my, oh my," she screamed angrily, as she hobbled away. "What is this land coming to?"

Tim was in Grandpa's shop when Mrs Plumme came wobbling in. Although Grandpa was very busy, he took pity on her and fixed the shoe right away.

"What do you think of all this, Mr Lambert?" she asked him. "It's a shame, isn't it?"

"Not at all," Grandpa said. "It's time people relaxed and stopped rushing about so much. Think of it as four weeks' holiday."

But Mrs Plumme was not amused. She paid for the shoe and sailed out of the shop.

"It's not funny, Grandpa," Tim scolded. "People have things to do. It's not fair for Prince Nat to do this. It's really not fair."

"Speaking of which," Grandpa said. "You should stop thinking about the fair so much. It will still be there when Prince Nat gets better. If not, next year. In the meantime, help your mother a little bit around the house."

"I'm always working," Tim said. "Nobody else works as hard as me."

"Doing what exactly, my boy?"

"Well," Tim tried to think of what he worked at, but nothing came immediately to mind. "Well, sometimes I wrap the flowers for Mama in the shop, and sometimes I help you to wrap and stack the shoes when you have a lot of work. And since Papa ... I've been taking the rubbish out."

"That's good," Grandpa smiled. "I'm proud of you, you know. Really I am. And your father would be, too."

"Grandpa, why did it have to be Papa?"

"I don't know, Tim. Sometimes it's just bad luck. But he wouldn't have wanted us to be sad. Remember that."

The bell on the shop's door tinkled as Mr Hicks clopped in for his repaired platform shoes. He had on a pink plastic jacket, white trousers, his green hat, and blue and orange platform shoes that looked brand new.

He, too, seemed enraged, and his red face now went with the rest of his clothes. "A nuisance, the whole lot of them," he grumbled as he handed his ticket to Grandpa.

"Who?" Grandpa asked.

"Kings, queens, princes, just a bunch of pests," Mr Hicks said.

"The Prince can't help it if he's ill," Grandpa said. "It's not his fault. It's probably that idiot of a Prime Minister who's responsible for all this."

"Well, he should've known better than to eat mussels," shouted Mr Hicks. "I know it's the national dish, but I, for instance, never touch them. Filthy little things in filthy shells."

Grandpa wondered if he ate anything at all, he was such a twig.

"We should get rid of the whole lot of them, except for the doctor-princess. At least she earns her keep," Mr Hicks mumbled as he walked out into the pouring rain.

Perhaps it was the rain as much as the Prime Minister's order that was putting some people in such a foul mood. If it had been sunny, the Natters would have just pretended they were on holiday. They would have taken their dogs walking, gone to the park to throw stones in the pond (the national sport), sat out on terraces drinking beer, or any number of things. But the rain prevented all that.

People hardly remembered any more what it was like to have two days of sunlight in a row. Now whenever the sun shone, you went to the Glacé Pyramid, had a quick ice cream, or in summer you rushed to the fair and afterwards waited for the rain to come back. And it invariably did.

But things hadn't been like that for ever. Natland hadn't always been wet. When Grandpa was a child, there had been whole weeks of sunshine in the spring, summer and even in autumn. The Natters would go to the beach in summer, or hiking in the woods in autumn. In winter, they went cross-country skiing or sleighing and had snowball-throwing contests. It used to be a fun-loving land of hearty men, laughing women and happy children.

But that was before the king with the grand ambitions came along – Natty the Dread, Prince Nat's grandfather. Long long before Tim was born, King Natty the Dread had grabbed himself a country in Asia named Gonghai, which had loads of diamonds, and he built huge monstrous castles all over Natland. He wanted his country to be the shining jewel of the continent and he wanted the Natters to be the richest people.

He told his subjects that they had to work harder, and that it was their right to have every new thing that came along. So the Natters were the first people to have cars, one per family, then two, then three. Later, when a baby was born, his first gift was a nice new convertible, which waited in the garage until he was old enough to drive it. King Natty the Dread had even invented a car himself, the Gnatbuggy in which he buzzed around Natland. The Gnatbuggy was shaped like a giant fruit fly, and it could whiz along at a mighty clip. It was still the most popular car in Natland, despite its nasty whine.

King Natty the Dread also built wide highways and massive bridges. He built high concrete towers. He tore down pretty old houses and put up colossal monuments to himself. All over Natland, there were statues of him sitting astride a mean-looking stallion.

During the reign of King Natty the Dread, the Natters had got richer and richer. They were the first people to have a telephone in every home, colour TV, washing machines, dishwashers, computers – you name it – they had it. They also get wilder and wilder about cars. The whole land became a racecourse. You know the saying "to drive like a natter"? That's where it came from. And they didn't like to drive on the left or the right of the road. No, everyone wanted to drive in the middle!

With all the fumes from the cars, the climate started changing while King Natty the Dread ruled. First, a little drizzle every day. Next, a real downpour two or three times a week. After that, rain for weeks on end. Then rain almost the whole year. Everyone said the cars were to blame with all their awful-smelling exhaust fumes, but even after Gonghai had a revolution and Natland started getting poorer, people held onto their cars. Even when King Natty the Dread died, the love of cars grew greater rather than less. So the rain continued, with everyone wishing it would go away and never come back. Because of the rain, the Natters all went around with long faces. The more it rained the longer their faces got.

When Prince Nat took the throne, he managed to undo a lot of the silly things his grandfather had done. He tore down the palaces and the ugly bridges. He tried, as well, to get rid of the stupid horse monuments, but Langi Lalla wouldn't hear of it, so the stone stallions stayed. Of the royal buildings, Prince Nat kept only one small castle for himself so he could entertain visiting VIPs who always expected a lot of pomp and circumstance.

Prince Nat had also tried to promote bicycles, but there he failed woefully because the Natters refused to give up their cars. (The Prince had to admit that he too liked a drive on the wild side, although he could barely see above the steering wheel). For the Natters, being deprived of their cars was the cruellest punishment.

But now that the Prince was ill, there were far fewer cars on the road, thanks to Langi Lalla. Would this make the rain stop for once?

Chapter
Five

Aunt Liana was not in a nice mood. She banged pots and pans as she went about her work. She shouted at Uncle Peter if he got in her way, although he was only trying to help. When her favourite salad bowl slipped out of her hands and crashed to the floor into a thousand pieces, she became even more vexed.

It was the rain that was causing it, and not being able to go out even for a drive. "Whatever am I doing in this nutty land?" she asked herself.

She was not the only one who was upset. All over Natland, people were steaming and feeling victimised, after a week of being stuck in their homes. Mothers and fathers yelled at each other and at their children. Sisters and brothers hurled insults at one another. Tim shouted constantly at Callaloo, and the parrot screamed back, "Get lost, get lost, get lost."

At the castle, Prince Nat grumbled and groaned and felt worse. Princess Soo Lian's pills were not doing him any good. Those bad mussels had poisoned his whole system, and he didn't even want to eat any more. Just the sight of food made him turn green. In a week he had lost two kilos, and the few muscles he had were shrinking.

Princess Soo Lian called in friends of hers who were experts in treating food poisoning, but no one knew what to do. They all shook their heads in bafflement that Prince Nat was sick for so long. What could have been in those mussels? Surely the sea wasn't that badly polluted?

By the second week, Natland was grouching, rumbling and fuming so much that the rest of the world thought a volcano was about to erupt. Only Prime Minister Langi Lalla was having the time of his life. It was all working out perfectly. Another week of this, he thought, and everyone would be ready to get rid of that shrimp Prince Nat. He went on the radio every day to remind people that as long as the Prince was sick, they had to stay put. And he watched in glee as bag-loads of letters arrived at the castle. At first they contained get-well cards, but later most were complaints about not being allowed to drive. One letter even told the Prince to abdicate if he couldn't get better.

Prince Nat tried to force Langi Lalla to stop the meanness, but he was too weak to do any good. Besides, Langi Lalla had paid a lot of people money so they wouldn't listen to the Prince any more.

He had also given a certain chef a nice little country home somewhere. The chef worked at Le Fish et Chips Restaurant, the very place where Prince Nat had eaten those mussels.

As Prince Nat showed no signs of getting better, people started fearing they might be stuck in their homes for months, which would drive them absolutely nuts. At the thought, even the children longed for school to begin so that at least they would have some escape.

Tim dreamed only of the fair. He spent his time drawing pictures of the Big Wheel, of the Magic Carpet which swung riders higher and higher into the sky until you screamed in fear, of bumper cars, of the roller-coaster. How he wished to ride them all.

Meanwhile in Slushigem, the fairground itself looked as if ghosts had taken over. No music, no movement, and all the rides covered in black plastic as the rain beat down. The people who owned the rides mostly came from other countries south of Natland and they all wanted to leave now, but they weren't allowed to pack up and drive off in their vans and trucks. So they too were steaming.

Then, on the morning of the fifth day of that second week, the rain stopped and the sun came out like a fireball. It was so bright that everyone had to put on dark glasses because they had got so used to the greyness. The people's spirits soared and they started making grand plans for outings and picnics. Tim and Cathy called Aunt Liana and got ready to go to the fair.

But on the news that morning, Langi Lalla said that sunshine or no sunshine, everyone still had to stay put. There would be no vehicles on the road except for those people who had special permission. Prince Nat was still ill.

People cursed and thumped and slapped their radios, they were so mad. Then they jumped in their Gnatbuggies and tried to drive off somewhere, anywhere, but Langi Lalla ordered the police to confiscate all car batteries. So the Natters were stuck again.

·······

In Tim's town, Sprinkleton, people gathered on the main square to decide what to do. To the surprise of many, Mr Hicks took control of the meeting, getting up on a bench to shout that the prince was a tyrant and that everyone should disobey the order to stay put. As he yelled, Mr Hicks looked like a giant bird from another planet. He had on blue-tinted glasses, a green shirt, red pants and the purple platform shoes.

Grandpa and Tim could see and hear the meeting from the shoe-repair shop and they noticed that people were cheering Mr Hicks and getting very worked up. Mrs Plumme, for instance, was jumping up and down in her high heels.

"Well, there's another pair of shoes to be fixed," Grandpa smiled at Tim.

"What's going to happen, Grandpa?" Tim asked.

"Oh, they'll cool down soon enough."

And he was right. As Mr Hicks reached a fever pitch in his speech, the skies darkened, and the rain came pelting down once more, sending the Natters scurrying indoors.

But the rain didn't completely dampen their temper. Some people were so hot under the collar that the windows of their homes got all steamed up, and the children amused themselves by writing "Wash Me" on the steam.

That evening Mr Hicks went clop-clopping around knocking on all the doors. He had a petition that he wanted everyone to sign. It said: "Beat it, Prince Nat". Some people signed in glee but others shooed him away. The petition gave rise to a lot of bad feeling, because when one family who was for the prince saw that their neighbours had signed, they went next door and spewed out insults, calling their neighbours "klunkhead", "goatbrains", "ratfink" and the like.

Soon the evening was thick with quarrels. People got into fistfights out in the rain and pushed one another down in the mud. They threw things at each other. The town's baker emptied a bag of flour all over Mr Hicks, and Mr Hicks threw one of his platform shoes at the baker, who luckily ducked just in time. People jumped into puddles and kicked dirty water in their neighbours' faces. When it was all over, everyone was muddied and bruised, and those against the Prince vowed never to talk again to those who were for him.

Chapter
Six

When morning came, the people of Sprinkleton felt only shame because deep in their hearts they were revolted by such fussing and fighting. In fact, the whole of Natland felt ashamed because similar fights had taken place all over the country. People were embarrassed to step out of doors because they didn't want to meet their neighbours' eyes.

Tim's mother, who had thrown a small pot of geraniums at Mrs Plumme, decided to make breakfast a lengthy affair so that she wouldn't have to open her shop and face people for at least another hour. She prepared pancakes, eggs, freshly squeezed orange juice, raisin muffins and hot chocolate. She called up to Tim and Cathy to wake up and come downstairs, and Cathy soon raced down. But not Tim.

"Tim, Tim, breakfast is ready," Mrs Lambert shouted up, but there was no answer. She went upstairs, saying, "Come on, it's time to get up. I've made pancakes and hot chocolate."

When she looked into Tim's room she found it empty, and he wasn't in the bathroom either. She went back into his bedroom and noticed a folded piece of paper on his pillow. It said: "Gone to the fair. Don't worry, Mama. Callaloo and I'll be back this evening."

Mrs Lambert ran downstairs and saw that Callaloo's cage was empty. She went to look out into the street, but not a soul was to be seen. When she told Cathy that Tim had gone off to the fair by himself, Cathy was hopping mad. How could he have left without her?

Mrs Lambert and Cathy rushed over to Grandpa's shop to ask him to go look for Tim. Grandpa was the only one in Sprinkleton who had dared to go about his business as usual because he hadn't taken part in the fights the night before.

"Oh, that boy, that boy," Grandpa muttered as he took off his blue apron and put on his raincoat and boots. "What are we going to do with him?"

He noticed that Mrs Lambert was close to tears, so he said, "Don't worry. I'll find him."

Right at that moment, Tim was walking down a back road with Callaloo on his shoulder. He sang as he trudged along, a popular song about King Natty the Dread. Callaloo joined in the chorus.

"King Natty the Dread,
What a big head, yeah."

Tim was in good spirits because he was going to the fair at last. He had a map in his plastic bag and figured he'd have to walk only a few hours before he got to Slushigem. Once he was there he'd go to Aunt Liana's house and ask her to take him to the fair.

Even if he couldn't get on the rides, he just wanted to see them. He remembered the last time he had been, when he was about seven. Papa had let him go on nearly all the rides except for the roller coaster. They had also gone into the House of Glass and fell down laughing when they saw how long their faces looked in the trick mirrors. Before they went home, Papa had entered one of those competitions where if you managed to knock down ten stacked tincans with a sponge ball, they gave you a big stuffed toy. Papa had won two toys – a bear for him and a pink fluffy dog for Cathy. The next year Papa was gone, after some Natter smashed into his car.

Tim walked and walked. It was tough going because King Natty the Dread hadn't bothered to pave these little back roads when he was building his grandiose highways, and Tim had to slosh through a lot of mud. The rain stung his face, making it difficult to see where he was going, and he tripped a couple of times. After an hour, he no longer felt like singing and, on his shoulder, Callaloo shivered and croaked, "Home, home, home."

"Be quiet," Tim muttered. "We're going to the fair."

Callaloo flew off his shoulder and went to perch on a branch just out of Tim's reach. His feathers were all wet. No one would have called him a pretty bird just now.

Tim jumped, trying to reach him, but Callaloo flew higher. The boy tried to climb up the tree but he slipped and fell into a big puddle of brown water which seeped under his raincoat and boots.

"Kyuk, kyuk, kyuk, kyuk," Callaloo laughed.

"Go on then," Tim yelled angrily. "Fly back home." He stalked off and Callaloo, preferring a free ride any day to long-distance flying, flapped after him and fluttered down on his shoulder.

By now Tim was shivering himself. Where was Slushigem? He sat down on a fallen tree trunk at the side of the road and took out his map. He had to be half-way at least after such a long walk, he thought. The rain soon soaked the map and when Tim tried to fold it up again, it came apart in his hands.

He clamped his jaws shut to keep from crying.

In Slushigem, Aunt Liana was on the phone with Mrs Lambert.

"Yes, yes. If he shows up here, I'll call you right away," Aunt Liana said. "And I'll tell Peter to go out to look for him."

Worry lines creased her face as she hung up. That poor child, out in weather like this. She told Uncle Peter what had happened and he quickly put on his raincoat and ran over to the house of a friend of his who was a firefighter.

Callaloo was getting wetter and wetter, and so was Tim.

"Ka-choo," sneezed the parrot, as he shivered even more. He had vague memories of sunshine, somewhere when he'd been a little chick.

"Home, home, home," he croaked.

"Look, I'll put you under my sweater," Tim told him. He bundled Callaloo under his pullover and although it was damp there as well, the parrot felt a bit better. He tried to shake out his feathers, but Tim wriggled and squealed, "Stop it, stop it! You're tickling me."

Callaloo closed his eyes and went to sleep as Tim tramped on. Finally, the rain eased and Tim could see more clearly. The road seemed endless; Slushigem was definitely not in sight. Soon he came to a fork in the road with signs pointing to the left and the right. One sign said, "Highway to Slushigem" and the other said "Floodington."

He walked to the highway, thinking he could perhaps hitch a ride from one of the people allowed to drive. His mother had told him never ever to hitchhike but Tim was so tired that he couldn't bear the thought of walking any further. The first thing he saw when he got to the highway was a blue mail-van racing down the middle of the road. He tried to wave it down but the driver apparently didn't see him. Next a bright red bakery van whizzed by, its wheels going through a puddle and splashing Tim from head to foot.

Now he couldn't keep back the tears. He was hungry, homesick and very wet. As he sat at the side of the highway crying, he heard a siren approaching. He looked up as a fire engine raced past, screeched to a stop and reversed. Before he could get up, Uncle Peter had jumped down and grabbed him in a bear hug, almost crushing Callaloo, who was still asleep.

"Where have you been, you silly boy?" Uncle Peter said. "Your mother is worried sick about you."

He put Tim between him and the driver in the cab of the fire engine and they drove off to Sprinkleton, siren screaming. On the way, they saw Grandpa and stopped to pick him up as well.

"Where have you been, you silly boy?" Grandpa asked. "Your mother is worried sick about you. Don't you know she'd die if she lost you too?"

In Sprinkleton, everyone came out to look as the fire engine stopped in front of the Lambert house. Tim had never felt so ashamed in his life. When he got down from the fire engine, his mother hugged him as hard as she could.

"Help, help, help," said a voice from under Tim's raincoat. It was Callaloo, who felt as if he was being smothered. Tim took him out and gave him to Cathy, while Callaloo blinked in the sudden light.

"Home, home, home," Callaloo croaked in joy.

Tim noticed that his mother's face was wet from crying.

"Sorry, Mama," he said. "I won't do it again. I just wanted to go to the fair."

"Did you go on any of the rides?" Cathy asked.

Tim didn't answer. He just wanted to go inside the house, away from all the prying eyes.

Chapter
Seven

Aunt Liana was as happy as a fly in a tripe shop. She'd received a telephone call from Uncle Peter saying that Tim was all right, and just now the mailman had brought her a telegram from Chaud'terre containing other splendiferous news.

"All coming to visit in three days' time. Hurricane heading this way. Can we bring you anything? Your brother King Tummy," the telegram said.

Aunt Liana couldn't stop smiling. It would be so nice to see her people once again after all this time. Of course it was really too bad about the hurricane, but if all the Chaud'terrians were coming to Natland, they would be out of danger from the 150-miles-per-hour winds. Everyone remembered the fierceness of Stormin' Norman, and some people were still rebuilding their homes months after it had passed through.

Aunt Liana especially looked forward to seeing King Tummy. Of her four brothers – Prince Tallalalawah, Count Cardinal, Duke Jumpup and King Tummy – he was her favourite. You see, Aunt Liana was from an important family in Chaud'terre. All her brothers were Boogalypso singers who made wonderful magic music. Every year, during the carnival, they brought the people so much joy that the Chaud'terrians had finally elected them to be the government.

From being Carnival King, Tummy had become Prime Minister of Chaud'terre. And a good one he was, too. All his speeches took the form of a Boogalypso song, and he had people in stitches whenever he came on the radio or TV.

Not only that, but King Tummy had discovered oil in Chaud'terre, lots and lots of oil, so that from being a rather poor country, Chaud'terre had got fabulously wealthy. But the people really didn't care much about money. The one thing that tickled their fancy was the carnival. After each hurricane, they had a magnificent carnival with everyone competing to see who could come up with the most outlandish costume, who could sing the best song and who could out-dance everybody else. King Tummy won every time.

In all, there were only 10,949 Chaud'terrians but what they lacked in numbers they made up for in spirit. They were a fun-loving people who learned to laugh even at hurricanes like Stormin' Norman.

Aunt Liana wrote out a little note to send back as a telegram. "Can't wait to see you. I don't need anything, except your latest records. And some mangoes and ginger. Love, Liana."

Then she started cleaning up the house. Of course, she wouldn't be able to put up all the Chaud'terrians but there was enough space for her brothers. She vacuumed every nook and cranny, and waxed all the furniture. She put fresh sheets on the beds, and changed the curtains. While she worked, she put on one of King Tummy's records.

"Wave your hands in the air.
Act like you just don't care.
Wave your hands in the air.
Shake your hips if you dare."

Later she walked in the drizzle down to the grocery store on the corner and bought loads of food for her brothers who had extremely hearty appetites.

Chapter
Eight

∙∙∙

Prince Nat was getting weaker and weaker. His stomach no longer hurt as much, but now he wouldn't eat. He couldn't stand the sight of food. Princess Soo Lian told the royal cook to take a holiday and she herself tried to make appetising dishes for Prince Nat, but he would take one glance at them and shake his head.

"Yuk," he said.

Princess Soo Lian tried everything. She gave him lichees in a pretty porcelain bowl, she gave him spring rolls, she gave him barbecued ribs, chow mein, fried rice.

"Yuk," he said to everything. Nothing could get his appetite back. One night, she woke him up and tried to get him to drink warm castor oil, which her granny used to say cured everything.

"Super yuk," Prince Nat said after the first sip, and wouldn't drink any more.

She tried all the medicine, new and old, that she knew. She tried yoghurt as well as Smith's Worm Medicine. She rubbed his chest with tiger balm and also made him steaming cups of camomile tea, but nothing worked. Prince Nat refused to eat. It's not that he didn't want to, but his stomach said *no* if he so much as looked at a potato chip. Even Princess Soo Lian could hear his stomach going *no-oh-oh-oh-oh*.

She didn't know what to do any more. If Prince Nat didn't start eating soon, he would waste away to nothing and she couldn't begin to imagine life without him.

Not only that, but there was talk of people storming the castle if they weren't allowed to move about as they wished. Princess Soo

Lian was getting afraid. She read and reread her medical tomes and her cookbooks, and kept on preparing mouth-watering dishes, but she ended up eating them all by herself. As Prince Nat got thinner, she got fatter.

When she wasn't cooking and taking care of the Prince, Princess Soo Lian spent her time reading and answering letters. More and more letters were arriving daily at the castle, some from royal relatives abroad who wanted to know what on earth was happening in Natland. There were also letters from VIPs who had been scheduled to visit and who now wondered whether it was convenient. Many get-well cards also came, along with letters that had some quite rude things about the Prince and Princess such as: *Prince Nat is a rat and his wife is a bat, she's getting fat while he's oh so flat, let's put them in a vat and leave it at that.*

What a bad poet, Princess Soo Lian thought, such atrocious rhymes. Still, the letter made her even more fearful and she realized something had to be done urgently. She put on her thinking cap – the red one – and sat down to work out a solution.

She had already begged Langi Lalla to permit the Natters to use their cars again. But he had dismissed her pleas with an imperious wave of the hand.

"I am the Prime Minister," he had said. "I am in control." Then he had tap-danced around his office, singing "Control, control. Woohoo, I'm in control." Princess Soo Lian had left in disgust.

What to do? What to do, she pondered. She wondered whether to ask for help from the King of Lowland, the neighbouring country of milk and cheese where everybody was over eight feet

tall. But Prince Nat couldn't stand the Lowians, who had looked down on his family for generations. So that was out.

Finally, she hit upon an idea. She would appeal directly to the Natters and give them something to occupy their minds while they were immobile.

Without Langi Lalla's knowledge she put a big advertisement the next day in all of Natland's newspapers. It said:

PRINCE NAT NEEDS YOUR HELP.
ANYONE WHO CAN COME UP WITH A DISH THAT WILL
MAKE HIM EAT AND GET STRONG AGAIN WILL BE
REWARDED WITH AN ALL-EXPENSES-PAID TRIP TO
A NICE HOT COUNTRY WHERE IT NEVER RAINS.
PLEASE BRING YOUR DISHES TO THE
ROYAL CASTLE ON FRIDAY.
PRINCESS SOO LIAN.

Langi Lalla was furious when he saw the advertisement, and out of spite he went on the radio to tell the Natters that they couldn't drive anywhere for an additional week. But since everyone had thrown away their radio because they'd got so tired of his annoying voice, no one heard the order. Besides, all the people could talk and think about was that advertisement in the newspaper. "Wouldn't it be wonderful," they asked one another, "to go far away to a sunny land where it never rains? To swim in the sea and dance under the stars? Wouldn't it, wouldn't it?"

As soon as they read the advertisement, everyone rushed to the grocer's to buy food and then rushed home to their kitchens to start cooking.

Even Cathy decided she'd try to make brownies for Prince Nat, so she called Auntie Liana for the recipe and spent hours mixing flour, chocolate, and nuts. She covered the whole kitchen with flour and burned all the brownies.

Grandpa locked up his shop and went home to cook chicken soup. He firmly believed it cured everything. When he was a child, that's what his mother had always made when he got ill.

All over Natland, people bent over pots and stirred and sweated. Some of the dishes ended up being half sweat and half food but people were too busy to notice. The whole country smelled like a restaurant and people from neighbouring lands felt their mouths watering and thought that Natland might not be such a bad place for a vacation, in spite of the rain.

Tim and Auntie Liana were the only ones who didn't get involved. Auntie was too busy preparing for her family, while Tim wasn't at all interested in going to any stupid hot country. All he wanted to do was go to the fair. In another week, it would be gone.

Chapter
Nine

The Chaud'terrians flew into Natland the day before the big cooking competition was to take place. As King Tummy stepped off one of the private jets that had brought them, the first thing he smelled was the Natters' cooking.

"My goodness," he said to his brothers. "Liana is really outdoing herself. What a scrumptious smell, eh?"

His brothers all nodded, pleased that Liana hadn't forgotten how much they appreciated her cooking. The four of them looked alike, but King Tummy was the tallest and Prince Tallalalawah the shortest. When they were children, King Tummy had always eaten twice as much as his brothers and that was how he had got his nickname. But because of all the dancing he did, he stayed slim, unlike Count Cardinal and Duke Jumpup, who both had potbellies that they were quite fond of.

Aunt Liana's brothers couldn't wait to see her, but they were going to have to stand in line for a long time because Natland's National Airport was packed from wall to wall. It was not only the Chaud'terrians who had arrived that day. People from everywhere were beating a path to Natland, drawn by the amazing smell of thousands of people cooking all at the same time. The visitors came from England, Wales, Scotland, Germany, Belgium, Spain, Ireland, France, and even as far away as Iceland. Only the people of Lowland refused to budge. "Sniff, sniff," they went, with their noses in the air. "What an awful smell. Whatever are those Natters up to?" The Lowians only liked milk and cheese.

Natland's National Airport was a tower of babble that day, with "Excusez-moi", "Danke schön" and "It's warm in here, isn't it?" all mixed together. The police had to work madly to keep people moving. They feared that a riot would break out if so many people were kept bunched together for too long. But they needn't have worried because all the travellers were in a smiling mood, dreaming of pies and puddings and other lovely things.

Of course, once the visitors were ushered outside the airport, they were stuck, as no taxis or buses were on the roads. There they stood in the rain with their bags and boxes, wondering if the transport workers were on strike. Suddenly Natland didn't seem so nice any more.

When King Tummy, his brothers and the other Chaud'terrians came out and saw the crowds getting soaked in the downpour, they all wished they had stayed home and faced the hurricane.

"My goodness," King Tummy said. "What a grey country!"

"Where are Liana and Peter? Aren't they coming to meet us?" Prince Tallalalawah wondered.

"Looks like the transport people are on strike. I'm so glad *we* don't have those problems anymore," Duke Jumpup said.

"Everybody looks so sad," Count Cardinal commented. "They need some cheering up bad."

The brothers nodded. They formed a little circle and whispered to one another. Then they looked again at the bedraggled people, getting wetter and wetter.

"All right, give me a beat," said King Tummy loudly.

"A-one, a-do, a-dree," shouted Count Cardinal.

"Never seen so much rain," King Tummy sang.

"Never seen so much rain," his brothers chorused.
"In all my life, never seen so much rain, don't want no Natland wife."
"No Natland wife," his brothers crooned.

"Never ..." King Tummy swallowed a mouthful of rainwater and coughed for several seconds. People stared at him. He thought for a bit and decided to get his parasol from his bag. When he was safely covered, he slapped his thigh with determination.

"OK," he said to Count Cardinal. "Give me another beat. Let's duet on this one, eh Duke?"

"A-one, a-do, a-dree," Count Cardinal said, and Prince Tallalalawah shouted, "Everybody, clap your hands."

King Tummy and Duke Jumpup started singing:

"Why you standing there looking so glum
Just because a little rain done come?
I say people give me half a chance
I ain't goin' stop till I make you dance!"

As the other Chaud'terrians saw their prime minister singing, they rushed to give him support. They opened their bags and took out tambourines and drums. Four or five people had guitars, and a few had flutes. They banged and strummed and blew in accompaniment. Soon, the other travellers started tapping their feet. Then they snapped their fingers. Some nodded their heads in time to the music. The daring ones twitched their hips – they weren't really used to this kind of music.

"Why you standing there looking so blue
Just because a little rain wet you?
This is Natland, a great place for fun –
So what if they never ever see the sun?"

"We still goin' dance, dance;
Come on people, let's dance!"

And what do you know? The crowd actually started swaying and
clapping their hands. Whenever King Tummy and Duke Jumpup

sang the chorus, everyone joined in: "*We still goin' dance, dance; Come on people, let's dance.*"

The police couldn't believe their eyes and ears. Was this a new kind of riot? People were bellowing with all their might, kicking their legs up in the air, swinging their hips from side to side and just acting plain crazy. Natland had never seen anything like it.

As they danced, the visitors began moving in the direction of Slushigem, pulled by King Tummy's masterly music.

"Why you stand there looking so fierce
Just because bus and taxi get scarce?
Let's all go to find a place to stay,
Even if Natland is rainy and grey."

"We still goin' dance, dance;
Come on people, let's dance!"

So they danced into Slushigem, making such a racket that all the
Natters thought a revolution was taking place. Some hid under
their beds, while others raced to their cellars, locking themselves
inside. As the crowd of dancing and singing people drew near to
the castle, Princess Soo Lian and Prince Nat prepared for the
worst. Prince Nat refused to hide and lay calmly under Great-
Aunt Magaretha's pretty blanket, while Princess Soo Lian
pushed furniture up against the bedroom door.

When Prime Minister Langi Lalla heard the approaching roar,
his grin was so wide that you could see all of his horse-like teeth.
"At last, at last," he chortled. "They're coming to get rid of that
wimp Nat."

So as to be safely out of the way when the mob arrived, Langi
Lalla screamed for his chauffeur and they both sped far away from
the castle in his big black Gnatbuggy.

Princess Soo Lian trembled more and more as the crowd grew
closer to the castle. What were the people singing? She couldn't
understand it. When the commotion was right in front of the
castle, she peeked through the curtains and saw people shimmying
and gyrating, kicking their legs up in the air and clapping their

hands. Some paused just long enough to snap a few pictures of the castle before dancing on.

Princess Soo Lian fainted and Prince Nat had to crawl out of bed to slap her cheeks. When she came to, she whispered, "Oh, Nat, your people have gone mad."

The crowd boogied on through Slushigem, getting smaller as some people jigged into the hotels along the way. By the time they reached the west end of Slushingem, where Aunt Liana lived, there were only about a dozen Chaud'terrians still singing.

Aunt Liana was just putting the finishing touches to a grand meal of roti, chick peas and stewed veggies when she heard the music. "Oh my goodness," she said to Uncle Peter. "Tummy, Cardy, Dukey and Tallalalawah are here already."

She went out to greet them, and when her brothers saw her they stopped singing and rushed over to envelop her in bear hugs. They slapped Uncle Peter on the back so hard that he almost fell to the ground.

"But Liana," King Tummy said, "what are you doing in this grey, wet land?"

Before Auntie Liana could answer, a burst of thunder roared across Natland like a drum roll.

"Tummy, Tummy," Aunt Liana said, her brown eyes filled with tears. "You brought me music."

They all went inside and had a gorgeous supper.

Chapter
Ten

The next morning, as if to make everyone forget the other 360 days of rain, the sun pushed aside all the clouds and blazed over Natland. People woke up early, with the feeling that something was different. They pulled back their curtains and grinned idiotically when they saw there was light everywhere. Natland shone and sparkled, and smelled of sausages and sprouts.

Before even taking off their pyjamas, the Natters all rushed to their kitchens to check on pots they had left simmering overnight with goodies for Prince Nat. They sniffed and stirred, and each person hoped his or her concoction would be the one to cure the prince.

Tim and Cathy were up early, like everyone else, and brimming with excitement about the trip. Cathy's brownies had finally come

out right, soft and chocolatey, and she could hardly wait for the Prince to bite into one. Tim had only one thought: if they were going to Slushigem, he would get to visit the fair, at last.

When the Lamberts were ready to leave the house, Grandpa came to get them, carrying a big pot of chicken soup. He took off the cover so they could all take a whiff.

"Mmmmm," Mrs Lambert said. "I couldn't have made it better myself."

"It smells delish, Grandpa," Cathy said.

Tim thought it smelled like old dishwater, but not wanting to hurt Grandpa's feelings, he muttered, "Mmmm, mmmm." Callaloo obviously thought that was funny because he immediately launched into a raucous "Kyuk, kyuk, kyuk." Grandpa smiled and tweaked the parrot's beak.

"You watch out now, you might have to drink some of this soup," he told Callaloo.

As the Lamberts set out, they were joined by their neighbours, balancing pots and pans on their heads. It was like a big parade or like an old-time market day. Everyone was in their Sunday best, although most people had the good sense to wear trainers or other comfortable shoes for the long trek to the castle. Mrs Plumme, of course, refused to give up her high heels, and she looked like a spinning top as she clacked along with her pot on her head. She had made cabbage soup for Prince Nat. At her side, Mr Hicks clopped on in his platforms. He was pot-less because he didn't even know how to fry an egg, but he carried a huge red notebook with him.

On the road, the people of Sprinkleton were joined by groups from other villages: from Floodington in the north, Squelchy-Ville in the south, Riverside in the east and Dripinvet in the west. They walked along, exchanging gossip about the Prince and Princess, and about what had made the Prince ill.

"I heard that Langi Lalla tried to poison him," an old man whispered to Grandpa.

"I wouldn't put it past that scoundrel," Grandpa said in disgust.

"Did you hear that Princess Soo Lian is getting rather chubby?" one Squelchy-Ville woman said to Mrs Plumme.

"It's about time," Mrs Plumme snorted. "I can't stand those twiggy types." Then she blushed bright red as Mr Hicks coughed offended beside her.

"What a lovely day it is today, eh?" someone else commented.

And Mrs Lambert said, "It's a bit too warm for me with this long walk." They were all dripping with perspiration after an hour.

Tim and Cathy walked with a group of other children who all wanted to carry Callaloo on their shoulders, but Tim refused to give him up although Callaloo probably wouldn't have minded the adventure. The children talked of nothing but the fair.

"The first thing I'm going on is the roller-coaster," Tim said.

"I'm going on the bumper cars," said Cathy. "They're my favourite."

"The Magic Carpet is the best ride of all," a red-headed boy declared. "It's only for the bravest."

"Oh, yeah?" countered a sturdy boy from Floodington. "I bet you you'll be too scared to get on the Whirl-a-Twirl."

"That's for babies," said the red-headed boy. And Callaloo cackled, "Kyuk, kyuk, kyuk."

They all began arguing about which ride was the scariest, whether it was the Big Wheel, which made your stomach jerk in fright when it began turning, or the train in the Ghost Tunnel, where horrible creatures leapt at you from the walls. Everyone had a favourite ride and thought the others were for sissies.

As the great crowd tramped towards Slushigem, dark clouds rolled over Natland, blotting out the sun.

"Oh no," everyone sighed. "Here comes the rain again!"

But it was only a slight drizzle that lasted for a few minutes before the sun struggled back through. It did make the road wet and slippery, though, so everyone had to walk more carefully. Only Mr Hicks had a bit of bad luck. A few miles from Slushigem, he slipped in his platform shoes, twisted an ankle and crashed to the ground, his pink trousers getting all muddied and his notebook getting wet. Several people gathered round in sympathy, but Mrs Plumme took charge. She handed her pot of cabbage soup to a friend, hoisted Mr Hicks on her shoulder and sailed on to Slushigem.

The walkers were all sweaty and tired by the time they got to the city but everyone was excited about the prize. Before heading for the castle, the Lamberts stopped at Aunt Liana's house so they could make the rest of the journey together. Aunt Liana's brothers were quite pleased to meet the rest of the family, and they were looking forward to the food extravanganza and to seeing Prince Nat. King Tummy planned to give the Prince and Princess an invitation to visit Chaud'terre, if he got close enough to them. After all, they were almost relatives because Prince Nat's Great–Aunt Magaretha had once ruled Chaud'terre, briefly.

For Aunt Liana, the trip to the castle was like the picnics she and her brothers used to go on long ago when they were children in Chaud'terre. Nearly every Sunday they would go to the gardens of

Queen Margaretha's Palace, which had been turned into a museum by then. In the grounds was a shop that sold coconut cake, guava cheese and mango ice cream, which their father would always buy for them after much pleading.

For today's outing, Aunt Liana had filled a picnic basket with a few of those long-remembered delights, which she planned as a surprise for her brothers as well as for Tim and Cathy.

When they got to the castle, they realized that all of Natland, plus a lot of tourists, were already there. People sat on the lawns around the building, perched in trees, squatted on the walls, stood on the pavement, and filled the surrounding streets. The Lamberts held onto one another and wriggled and squeezed until they reached the castle lawn. From there, they managed to burrow their way up until they were in the fourth row. In front of the crowd, sitting side by side on a platform, were Prince Nat and Princess Soo Lian – one small and short, the other tall, beautiful and plumper than they remembered her from pictures in the newspapers.

Beside the platform stood several of the castle workers, dressed in red shirts and green breeches, with a black sash across their chests. They had microphones through which they kept on saying, "Those with food, please form a line. Prince Nat will taste your dishes one by one. If you have no food for the Prince, sit by the wall. Those with food, please form a line. When you get to the front, announce your dish. Let the tasting begin."

People with pots and pans jostled to get in line, wanting to be the first to hear Prince Nat say, "How delicious, I'm cured." But, of course, it wasn't going to be that easy. Cathy, Mrs Lambert and Grandpa joined the queue while Tim, Uncle Peter and Aunt Liana and her brothers inched their way over to sit under a walnut tree.

The first in the queue was a man from Floodington, who said his name was Jack Le Sausse.

"And what have you cooked, sir?" bellowed the chief castle staffer.

"Fried blood-sausages for His Majesty," Jack Le Sausse bellowed back.

"Approach and let the Prince taste it."

The man went up to Prince Nat, bowed, and stretched forth a fork with a fat brown sausage on the end.

Prince Nat's face turned the same shade of green as his workers' shirts.

"Yuk," he said.

And from the somewhere on the lawn came an echo of "Kyuk, kyuk, kyuk," as Callaloo chuckled.

Jack Le Sausse bowed his head and lost himself among the crowd, which had got as still as a church congregation.

"Next," yelled the chief castle staffer.

The following person was an old woman from Dripingvet, who said her name was Mrs Katy Cornfield.

"And what have you got, Madame?"

"Tripe and beans," the old lady said proudly. She held a brimming pot in front of Prince Nat, and he clutched his stomach and said, "Super yuk."

"Kyuk, kyuk, kyuk," Callaloo cackled.

The third entrant was, lo and behold, Mrs Plumme, who had pushed her way past everyone else.

"I have something that will cure His Majesty Prince Nat," she announced boldly, so everyone could hear.

"And what might that be?" the chief castle staffer asked.

"Cabbage soup. Just take a little sip, Prince Nat," she said coaxingly, waving a spoonful of yellow liquid under his nose.

Prince Nat hesitatingly took a taste, and began sputtering and coughing.

"Mega-mega yuk," he shouted.

"Kyuk, kyuk, kyuk," Callaloo went, as Mrs Plumme flounced off angrily.

Tim tried to subdue the parrot by putting him under his shirt, but Callaloo screeched so loudly and made such a terrible racket that Prince Nat stared in Tim's direction. To stop the noise, the boy had to put Callaloo back on his shoulder. As person after person went up and was dismissed by the Prince, Tim began getting bored … and hungry.

"Can't we eat something, while we wait for Mama, Grandpa and Cathy?" he asked Aunt Liana.

"Of course, dear," Aunt Liana said. "I have a real treat for you, too."

Out of her picnic basket, she took first a cone and then a white plastic ice bucket. As Tim watched curiously, she scooped two balls of orange-coloured ice cream onto the cone.

"Whoopee," Tim yelled. "Mango ice cream."

"Me too, me too," said Uncle Peter, King Tummy, Duke Jumpup, Count Cardinal and Prince Tallalalawah. So Aunt Liana had to fix a cone for each of them and then one for herself.

They all sat under the tree, licking away contentedly as Prince Nat grew grumpier and grumpier. Soon it was Grandpa's turn to offer him some chicken soup and all the Lamberts held their breath as the prince gingerly took a sip.

"Yuk," he said. "Dishwater." So poor Grandpa, flushing with disappointment, had to take away his pot.

Then Cathy went up, with Mrs Lambert beside her for company.

Prince Nat stared long and hard at the brownies until Princess Soo Lian gave him a nudge. He took one and bit off a tiny piece. His face brightened somewhat. He bit off another piece, a bigger one.

"Mmm, not bad," he said. "But way too sweet."

"Next," roared the chief castle staffer, as Cathy tearfully went to sit beside Tim and the others.

Just then, someone limped up to stand before the royal platform. It was Mr Hicks.

"All this bad food will never cure you," he announced to Prince Nat. "What you need is sustenance for the soul. You need poetry."

Prince Nat and Princess Soo Lian looked at one another in bafflement, wondering who the strangely dressed fellow was, while the people of Sprinkleton turned their eyes away in embarrassment. Drawing himself up to his full height, Mr Hicks opened his battered red notebook and began reciting at the top of his lungs:

"There once was a prince named Nat
Who was as scrawny as an alley cat.
This prince was a real wimp,
He ate only mussels and shrimp,
Which made him as sick as a rat."

As he recited, people stared in horror, waiting for the castle workers to drag him off to a dungeon or something like that. Open-mouthed, they looked at the Prince, wondering what he would do. But Prince Nat was grinning broadly. He slapped his little thigh and roared, "Ha, ha, ha. More, more." But Princess Soo Lian was frowning, she thought this bad poetry sounded rather familiar, like some of the letters she had been getting.

Feeling full of confidence, Mr Hicks read another verse:

"As Prince Nat lay in bed and grew thin,
He committed Natland's worst-ever sin:
Like a mean old thuggy
He said we couldn't drive our Gnatbuggy
And so everyone had to stay in."

"That's not true," Prince Nat shouted. "It's Prime Minister Langi Lalla who did that. I would never have done anything like that. Where is he, anyway? Where is that donkey?" As he glared around looking for Langi Lalla, Mr Hicks' confidence seeped away and he tried to move quickly back into the crowd, but tripped in front of the platform as he went.

"Kyuk, kyuk, kyuk," Callaloo laughed, while Mrs Plumme rushed to rescue Mr Hicks.

Prince Nat looked in the parrot's direction and saw the Lambert family licking at their ice cream.

"You boy, with the parrot, come here," he summoned Tim.

Tim went timidly up to the platform.

"What are you eating?"

"Mango ice cream, Prince Nat, sir," Tim answered. "My Auntie Liana made it."

"Let me taste it. How come nobody brought me some?"

Tim reluctantly handed over his ice-cream cone and Prince Nat licked at it. Then he took a big bite, right through the cone. Crunch, crunch, went his teeth. Before Tim could count to ten, his whole ice-cream cone was gone.

"What's your name?" Prince Nat asked. Tim told him, and the prince said, "Does your auntie have any more ice cream?"

So Tim went over to Aunt Liana for another ice cream cone and carried it to the prince, who downed it in no time.

"Delicious," he said. "I'll have to tell them to make this flavour at the Glacé Pyramid next time. You're a good boy. That's a funny bird you have there. What's his name?"

"Callaloo," Callaloo answered before Tim could reply. "Kyuk, kyuk, kyuk."

Prince Nat whispered something to Princess Soo Lian, who asked one of the castle staffers for a microphone.

"Tim Lambert and his Auntie Liana are the winners of our competition," she announced. "He's made the prince eat again, hip, hip hooray."

All the Natters yelled, "Hip, hip, hooray!"

"Where do you want to go?" Princess Soo Lian asked Tim. "What nice sunny country would you like to visit?"

"I only want to go to the fair," Tim said, while his mother and Grandpa gestured wildly, trying to make him name some exotic place. "My sister and I couldn't go before because you were sick."

"Only the fair?" Princess Soo Lian asked. "Don't you want to go far away to some little island where it never rains?"

"No," Tim said. "I only want to go to the fair."

Grandpa and Mrs Lambert held their heads in dismay.

"Well, let's all go to the fair, then," Prince Nat said. "But first, let's meet this wonder aunt of yours and have a little chat."

While the people in Slushigem were enjoying what had turned out to be a huge picnic, Prime Minister Langi Lalla was choking on his own rage at his seaside mansion.

He'd last been in Slushigem when the Chaud'terrians had arrived, and he had raced away from the castle convinced that a revolution was going to take place. Now he was hopping mad because he had just heard on the news that Prince Nat was still very much on the throne, and not only that, but he was eating mango ice cream.

"Imagine that!" Langi Lalla screamed, pulling at his tuft of hair. "His wonderful Majesty is eating mango ice cream. Mango ice cream, after all my hard work to get rid of the wimp!"

Langi Lalla ran around his house in a rage, overturning tables and throwing precious ornaments against the wall. *Clapash!* went a terribly expensive porcelain vase. *Baplunk!* went a gold trophy he'd won years ago in a competition. *Boodoomp!* went a wooden elephant he'd received from the King of Bacanda.

His chauffeur Jonathan, who was also in the house, shuddered with fear in a corner.

"Come here, you quivering insect," Langi Lalla yelled at him. "We're going to Slushigem *now.*"

The chauffeur rushed out to start the Gnatbuggy, and Langi Lalla followed, heaving his bulk onto the back seat and slamming the car door hard.

With an ear-splitting whine, the Gnatbuggy jerked and set off, speeding to Slushingem. It flew past the rain-washed houses on the

coast, which soon disappeared in the distance. It sped past statues of King Natty the Dread on his stallion, to which Langi Lalla gave a respectful salute.

"Ah, Natty, if only you were still here," the Prime Minister said with a tear in his eye. "That grandson of yours is destroying our lovely Natland."

The car raced past cows, sheep and horses, grazing in the fields. It went round the famous hill of Slideville, which had been the scene of a fierce battle long ago between the Natters and the Lowians, over whose cheese was smellier. It whizzed past pigs rolling around in the mud, past shining ponds and lakes, and gardens filled with roses and azaleas that Langi Lalla didn't even notice.

When the chauffeur slowed down for a red light, Langi Lalla slapped him on the back of his head, yelling, "Step on it, go, go, you son of a donkey."

For the whole journey, the Prime Minister was so angry that his snorts steamed up the windows of the Gnatbuggy. The poor chauffeur had to keep wiping the inside of the windscreen so that he could see where he was going.

In the back seat, Langi Lalla clenched his jaws and tried to figure out a surefire way of getting rid of Prince Nat. He wasn't going to give up now. All his life he had got what he wanted and this time wouldn't be any different, he vowed. He thought about all the successes he had had, from the time he was a boy to when he became Prime Minister.

It was in school long ago that he had developed his purring/braying voice. In class, when he didn't do his homework and the teacher demanded to know why, he would purr, "Oh, I'm so sorry, Miss. I was taking care of my sick grandmother. She has to stay in bed, so I've been sitting beside her every evening, reading to her and helping her to eat."

And the teacher's eyes would get all soft and misty, as she said to the rest of the class, "Now, that's a good example to follow, everyone."

Of course, Langi Lalla's grandmother was fitter than a soldier and she ruled the family home like a general.

Another time, Langi Lalla would purr, "I'm sorry I couldn't do my homework, but my pet boa constrictor got out of the house and I had to spend all evening looking for him because he is very dangerous." That wasn't true either. He did have a guinea pig that he was very mean to, but he lied that he had a big snake so all the other children would be even more afraid of him.

They already feared him because he was a bully in the playground. He went about braying and picking fights with boys smaller than himself. Whenever anyone complained about him to the principal, Langi Lalla would just turn on his purr and look as innocent as a one-week-old kitten.

At home, his favourite game was going up to the top floor of the house and throwing his sister's toys down to the terrace below. It thrilled him to hear them crash against the tiles. If his mother and father scolded him, he would just grin as soon as their backs were turned. Only his grandmother could get him to behave. She made him stand in a corner and threatened to whip him with a cane if he budged.

When Langi Lalla went to university, he didn't change very much. He still gave outrageous excuses for not doing his homework, and he managed to push his way into leadership of a lot of groups such as the debate club, the car-racing team and the stone-throwing squad. Right after he graduated, his father got him a job as second assistant to the secretary of King Natty the Dread, but that was not enough for Langi Lalla. He wanted to be the King's right-hand man, so he began doing sneaky little things like changing words in important documents and blaming it on the secretary. When the secretary wrote, for intance, "The King will speak to the Nursing Club," Langi Lalla stealthily changed it to: "The King will squeak to the Cursing Club," and so on. Finally King Natty the Dread fired his secretary and promoted Langi Lalla to the position.

Langi liked and respected the king, who was an even greater bully than he. And King Natty the Dread was quite fond of Langi because the young bully did everything the King commanded. It took only a short time for Langi Lalla to become a big-shot in Natland. Soon he was on TV and radio, chatting away and promising to do this and that for the Natters. And he travelled all over the country, kissing babies and whispering sweet nothings in people's ears. He charmed so many people that they elected him to be the next Prime Minister. But he wanted more. When King Natty the Dread died after falling from his horse, Langi Lalla had grand dreams of being made king, but little Prince Nat soon put a stop to that.

"Ah, that louse," Langi Lalla muttered to himself now as the Gnatbuggy entered Slushigem and headed for the castle. "He's been such a royal pain in the neck. But no more. No more."

He wiped steam off the window and looked out as the Gnatbuggy slowed to a crawl. There were people everywhere, blocking the car's progress.

"Blow the horn, you fool," Langi Lalla yelled at the chauffeur. "Let them get out of our way."

The chauffeur sounded the horn, long and loud, but while a few people tried to make space, most ignored the big black Gnatbuggy. Langi Lalla rolled down his window, stuck his head out and brayed angrily, "Move, move, you idiots."

"Oh, it's the Prime Minister," someone said. "Let him through."

The words echoed among the crowd and people moved aside to let the car pass. Langi Lalla glared at everyone as he went by.

But as he approached the castle, the crowd was so dense that there was no way the Gnatbuggy could keep going.

"Drive on, drive on, you nincompoop," Langi Lalla said. But the chauffeur had had enough.

"Drive it yourself, bighead," he retorted, turning off the engine. He got out of the car, slammed the door and stalked off into the crowd.

"Come back here, you come right back here," Langi Lalla shouted after the chauffeur's disappearing form. But the chauffeur didn't even look back. Langi Lalla was left stranded in the Gnatbuggy.

He sat there for a minute choking on his rage, then he too got out of the car and pushed his way through the crowd. "I'm the Prime Minister. Move aside, move aside at once," he brayed. "Where's Prince Nat?"

People hesitantly gave way, pointing in a certain direction, and Langi Lalla managed to reach an area of the crowd that wasn't so tightly packed. There, sitting under a tree and talking with some strange people and ... a parrot! ... were Prince Nat and Princess Soo Lian. Langi Lalla barged right up to them.

"Oh Langi, where have you been?" Prince Nat greeted him. "I've told the people about your little trick. So let's get back to business now and stop all this rubbish, eh? In the meantime let me introduce you to ..."

"It's all over," Langi Lalla interrupted. "I'm taking control from now on. You're finished."

"Excuse me?" Prince Nat said politely. "What are you talking about?"

"You'll see," Langi Lalla said between clenched teeth. He sprinted over to the platform on which Prince Nat had earlier sat and grabbed a microphone.

"My beloved Natters, my dear friends, I have good news," he gushed. "Listen to me."

People stopped eating and talking, and looked up at Langi Lalla, wondering what was coming. They didn't trust him any more after what Prince Nat had said.

"Our good Prince Nat has decided to abdicate in repentance for all the pain he has put you through," Langi Lalla said. "From now on, I'm your sole leader. I will rebuild all of Natland's beautiful palaces. I will invade Gonghai and make it ours again. I will tear down that ugly Glacé Pyramid and build the greatest statue yet of King Natty the Dread in its place. I will insist that more cars be made. I know how happy you must be."

But nobody clapped or cheered. The people just stared at him.

"Long live Langi Lalla," someone finally shouted. It was Mr Hicks. "Long live our Prime Minister."

Langi Lalla beamed, waiting for others to take up the cry, but no one else did. And Mr Hicks soon grew quiet as Mrs Plumme slapped a hand over his mouth.

As Langi Lalla stood there, looking around desperately, one of the men with whom Prince Nat had been talking came over to the platform.

"Give me the mike," the man said to Langi Lalla.

"What? Who are you?"

"I am the Prime Minister of Chaud'terre, and I don't want my sister living in a country ruled by a nutter," the man said. It was King Tummy, of course. He got up beside Langi Lalla and took the microphone from him. But Langi Lalla snatched it back.

"Go away," he brayed. "I'm the ruler here. I want you out of my country right away. Police! Get this man."

But King Tummy only laughed and began singing:

"Is this your prime minister?
Oh, he's looking so sinister.
Is this the ruler of the land?
He's so fierce, I 'fraid to shake his hand."

"Oh Mister Prime Minister, what is your game?
In your place, I'd be feeling full o' shame.
Mister Prime Minister, you're starting to look pale:
Better run away before we throw you into jail!"

How the Natters chortled! And Callaloo the parrot "kyakked" loudest of all. Langi Lalla stood there swollen with rage, while his people joined King Tummy for a chorus of *"Oh Mister Prime Minister, what is your game? In your place, I'd be feeling full of shame."*

But Langi Lalla really had no shame. "Stop! Stop!" he commanded. "Listen to me. I will make Natland great again, just like King Natty the Dread. You'll have everything you want. You can drive your cars again. In fact, I'll give everyone a free car. We'll be the greatest land in the whole wide world."

But the Natters weren't fooled. They just kept singing, *"Oh, Mister Prime Minister, what's your game?"* And when they got bored with that, some people shouted, "To jail with him."

But Prince Nat had a better idea. He went up to the platform and signalled for quiet. "Langi Lalla, you have gone too far this time," he said to the Prime Minister. "You've forced me to take action."

The crowd grew terribly silent, and even Langi Lalla was speechless for a moment.

"Do you have anything to say before I pronounce your punishment?" Prince Nat asked.

"Punishment? What punishment, you imbecile?" Langi Lalla screamed. "I am the Prime Minister. The people *love* me. Me, me, me. Besides, I haven't done anything wrong."

Prince Nat turned to the crowd. "What shall we do with him?" he asked simply.

While the crowd whispered and pondered, a short fat man suddenly came forward, his jowls quivering in fear as he approached the prince.

"Your Majesty," he said. "I have something to confess."

Prince Nat peered at him, wondering where he had seen him before. "Yes? Come up on the platform."

"Your Majesty," the man said, going up and glancing uneasily at Langi Lalla who glared back. "I am the cook at Le Fish et Chips Restaurant. I made you sick from those mussels. Mister Langi Lalla ordered me to put something in the sauce."

"It's a lie," Langi Lalla shouted. "I'll rip you apart, you piece of blubber." He tried to get at the cook, but King Tummy blocked his way.

Soon other people were coming forward with more tales of Langi Lalla's treachery.

"He told me to put pepper in your coffee," one said. "But I didn't do it, Your Majesty."

"He once ordered me to put worms in Princess Soo Lian's shoes," a castle worker said. "And he fired me when I didn't."

"He paid me to steal your papers. And I'm so sorry, so sorry," another man said, crying his eyes out.

"Okay, enough. I've heard enough," Prince Nat said. The crowd grew quiet again.

"Langi Lalla," Prince Nat thundered, "I hereby banish you forever to Lowland. Don't ever come back."

Langi Lalla felt as if a rock had fallen on his head. He'd never expected this. "No, no," he began blubbering. "Not to Lowland. Don't send me to Lowland, please. I can't stand that cheesy smell. Nooooo." As the Prince's guards grabbed hold of him, he tried to put up a fight, kicking out his size-fifteen feet and flailing his arms.

"I'll get you for this, you wimp," he screamed. "I'll come back and make you sorry. I'll get you, I'll get you, I swear." The guards hauled him away.

Prince Nat looked at the crowd, sweeping his eyes over their faces, then staring straight at the brightly dressed Mr Hicks. "Is there anyone who wants to go to Lowland with Langi Lalla?"

Mr Hicks cowered and said nothing.

"Okay then." Prince Nat turned to King Tummy and gave him a friendly slap on the thigh. "Come on, man. Let's all go to the fair now," he said.

Chapter
Twelve

The people who ran the fair couldn't believe their ears when they heard the approaching commotion. Was it their lucky day at last? Were the Natters coming to the fair? Was the Prince better?

As they rushed to remove the black plastic that covered the rides, two of Prince Nat's staffers arrived with megaphones to announce that, yes indeed, the Prince and many, many Natters were on their way.

"Get the rides ready, it's fun-time, fun-time, fun-time," blared the megaphones.

The fair people ran about excitedly, fixing up their stands and starting the music. They put on disco songs by those old favourites – Bertha Blue and the Bluesettes, P.C. Hammer and the Nails, Pineapple Delight All Right and the world-famous Jammin' Jackson. Each ride had its own sound. At the bumper cars, the voice of Bertha Blue filled the air with "Let's do the bump, bump, yeh, let's do the bump, bump, yeh." And at the fortune-teller's stall, a group from long long ago sang, "I wanna hold your hand." The CD sounded scratched.

Meanwhile the crowd drew nearer and nearer. Prince Nat and Princess Soo Lian were walking at the head of the pack, along with the Lambert family and Aunt Liana and her brothers. Tim, with Callaloo on his shoulder, walked beside the Prince, who chatted about his Great-Aunt Magaretha.

"Isn't that funny?" Prince Nat said to Tim. "When I was your age, I thought my great aunt was a real nut with all her talk about this country called Chaud'terre. Now here I am, saved by your aunt who is from that place. She makes the best ice cream I've ever tasted. Do you think she'll invite us to dinner sometime?"

"No dinner, no dinner," Callaloo screeched.

"You'll have to ask her," Tim said to the Prince. Somehow he wasn't very keen to share Aunt Liana's specialities with anyone else. But then he realized it was mean to think like that. So he said, "She also makes nice cookies, and patties, and lemonade, and chips, and chocolate cake and everything. Mama says she's the best cakerer, I mean caterer, in Natland."

"Mmmmmm," Prince Nat said, licking his lips. "I hope she'll invite me and Princess Soo to dinner."

"I'll ask her," Tim declared.

"By the way, you can still take that prize Princess Soo promised, you know. You can go to a nice warm country with beaches and lovely fruit and things like that. Have you ever been with your aunt to Chaud'terre?"

"No, but she says she'll take me one day. We were supposed to go before but then my father was in an accident and we couldn't go."

"Oh, I'm sorry to hear that," Prince Nat said. "Is your father okay now? He didn't come today, did he?"

"No, he died in the accident," Tim explained in a shaky voice. "A crazy driver crashed into his car."

"Oh, I'm so sorry. Everyone drives so badly in our country. I'm going to do something about it, I promise you. Maybe I'll try again with those bicycles."

After a short silence, he asked, "Do you have a bicycle? No? We'll have to get you one, then."

"Can I have a mountain bike, please?" Tim pleaded. "Instead of the prize?"

"Mmmm," the Prince stroked his chin. "I don't see why not, even though there are no mountains in Natland. We'll give you the bike as a bonus, how's that? And when you go to Chaud'terre, I think I'll come along."

"Yeahhhh!" Tim said.

While the Prince and Tim chatted, Aunt Liana was divulging to Princess Soo Lian her secret recipe for mango ice cream. The Princess wrote it all down, then she went over to whisper something to Prince Nat. A moment later, she asked Aunt Liana: "Would you please make mango ice cream at the Glacé Pyramid on the next sunny day?"

"I'd be delighted," Aunt Liana said, beaming with pleasure.

When they got to the fairground, the rides were all ready and the whole place was swinging. Mrs Lambert gave Tim and Cathy money for the rides and the family agreed to meet later at the Magic Carpet. The children raced immediately for the Whirl-a-Twirl.

"Hang on tight, Callaloo," Tim yelled, as they were spun round and round and up and down for the next five minutes. Callaloo was cross-eyed by the time they got off.

They tried next to get on the bumper cars, but the line stretched for miles because all the Natters wanted a chance to drive. It had been so-o long, it seemed, since they'd been in a car. Tim and Cathy gave up and went on the Log-Slide instead, riding in little log-shaped boats down a chute that ended in a pool of water. They got splashed and Callaloo croaked in annoyance as he shook out his feathers. Without Tim noticing, he flew off.

Everyone was having a ball. Prince Nat and Soo Lian were on the roller coaster, screaming in fear as it plunged down, sped uphill and dived again. Mrs Lambert was throwing darts at balloons, jumping up and down and clapping her hands every time she burst one.

Over at the Stone-the-Duckies stall, Mr Hicks was hurling little rubber balls at yellow plastic ducks. He hoped to win a prize to impress Mrs Plumme – who stood nearby watching him and eating a candy apple – but his aim was terrible. Each time he missed, the stall-owner grinned broadly. Mrs Plumme, her face quite sticky from the apple, frowned.

Meanwhile, Grandpa and Uncle Peter were at the shooting gallery, firing pellets at a target and frequently hitting the little black centre.

"Whoopee," yelled Grandpa. "Bullseye!"

They had already won an elephant and a lion, and the stall-owner's face was red with irritation.

Count Cardinal and Duke Jumpup were in the Hall of Mirrors, laughing hysterically as they struck different dancing poses and the mirror twisted the images. King Tummy and Prince Tallalalawah were sampling some Natland specialities – chips dipped in honey and spicy fried snails (which the Natters called "Earth-fish").

"Dee-licious," King Tummy said, munching away.

Aunt Liana decided to have her palm read and went into the fortune-teller's tent. Behind a little round table sat a tall woman wearing a red turban, big gold earrings and a long black dress. She

had a huge piece of cheese attached to a silver chain around her neck.

"Hello," she greeted Aunt Liana in a deep voice. "Don't mind the cheese. It's just to ward off bad luck." She had a Lowian accent.

Aunt Liana sat down and the fortune teller took her hand. She furrowed her brow and stared at the lines on Aunt Liana's palm.

"You're going to meet a tall, handsome stranger from a cold, rainy land," she began.

"I am married to him," Aunt Liana said.

"Oh yes. I see that now," the fortune-teller said, frowning at the interruption. "You are going to travel soon to a distant land, with palm trees and lots of sunshine, and you'll have a little boy with you, and a ... I think, a chicken. No, a pigeon. Some kind of bird."

"Could it be a parrot?" Aunt Liana asked helpfully.

"If you say so," the fortune-teller answered frostily. "Where was I? Yes, I also see you in a big kitchen, cutting up fruit, apples I think. No, pears."

"Maybe mangoes?" suggested Aunt Liana.

"Whatever you like," the fortune-teller said, stretching out her hand for her money. "That will be ten Natbucks."

"Boy, I can tell better fortunes than that," Aunt Liana muttered to herself as she left the tent. She went over to the shooting gallery to meet Uncle Peter and Grandpa, who were firing their last pellets. Uncle Peter proudly gave her the lion he had won, and they all went looking for the rest of the family.

Tim and Cathy were still going from ride to ride, only stopping for candyfloss and chocolate-covered pears. It wasn't until they were on the Big Wheel, looking out at the Glacé Pyramid, that Tim suddenly realized Callaloo was not on his shoulder, and probably hadn't been for some time.

"Oh no, oh no, oh no," he thought, imagining the parrot caught between the wheels of one of the rides or drowned on the Log-Slide. He couldn't wait to get off the Big Wheel.

When they were back on the ground, he told Cathy that Callaloo was missing and they both pushed their way through the crowds to the Magic Carpet, where they'd agreed to meet the others. Mrs Lambert was already there waiting for them, and soon Grandpa, Aunt Liana and Uncle Peter walked up.

"Don't worry," Grandpa said, when he heard the news. "We'll find that silly bird."

"He's not silly, Grandpa," Tim protested. "He's a very smart bird."

They began searching for Callaloo, going from ride to ride and asking people if they'd seen a parrot. No one had. They looked up in the air, hoping they'd see him flying by or even perched on the roof of a stall. No luck. They ran into King Tummy and his brothers who also joined the search, looking in the Ghost Tunnel and in the House of the Lion-Man. But Callaloo was nowhere to be found.

After a while, the Lamberts met Prince Nat and Princess Soo Lian and they too offered to lend an eye in the search. Other people stared at the group as they went about the fairground calling "Callaloo, Callaloo!"

When they had looked at almost every stall and ride, they became convinced that the parrot had been reduced to a couple of green or red feathers by then. But no one wanted to say that to

Cathy and Tim. They had reached the farthest end of the fairground and Grandpa was just about to call off the search, when they heard a voice shouting:

"Come on up, try your luck. For one Natbuck, try your luck."

It was a hoarse voice that sounded most familiar.

"That's him," Tim cried. "Let's go."

They elbowed their way through a laughing mass of people who were crowded round a stall. There, basking in all the attention, was Callaloo. He was perched on a box on top of the stall's counter, inviting people to lift a block of iron so they could win a barrel full of mussels. A stout man, in a sailor's cap, stood behind the parrot.

"Test your muscles. Get some mussels," the man said, patting his big paunch. And Callaloo repeated the words, making the people giggle.

"You there, shorty," the man said, pointing at Prince Nat. "Wanna win some mussels?"

"No, thanks," the prince said coldly. "And that's Prince Nat to you, Mister Tubby."

As the man stood there with his mouth wide open, Tim shouted, "That's my bird. What are you doing with him?"

"'Allo, 'allo," Callaloo said, cheerily.

"Oh, it's your parrot, is it?" the man in the sailor's cap said, peering at Tim. "Well, he flew onto my counter and I fed him a few chips and he decided to stay and help me out. I must say he's a very fast learner. How much do you want for him?"

"He's not for sale," Grandpa spoke up. "He's coming back with us."

"Okay, okay. Keep your shirt on," the man said. "But I'm going to miss that bird. He brought me a lot of business." He stroked Callaloo's feathers, and the bird pecked at his hand.

"Now don't be naughty," scolded the man. "Here's another chip before you go."

Callaloo took the chip in his beak and flew down onto Tim's shoulder.

"'Allo, 'allo," he said and the chip fell to the ground.

"You dumb bird," Tim grinned. "We've been looking all over for you. We're going home now."

As he spoke, a big drop of water fell on his cheek. He looked up, and another drop plopped on his nose.

The rain had started again in Natland.